The Bureau of Substandards Annual Report

Sabrina Chase

Cover art and design by Chris Stewart

ISBN-13: 978-1-940006-02-4

CONTENTS

Acknowledgments   i

1   The Inspection   1

2   The Correct Way to Fill Out Form PCR-103-u   14

3   Read This Memo   33

4   Where the Money Went   40

5   All According to Regulations   53

Also by Sabrina Chase

Firehearted
The Last Mage Guardian

THE SEQUOYAH TRILOGY:
The Long Way Home
Raven's Children
Queen of Chaos

The Scent of Metal

ACKNOWLEDGMENTS

The extremely talented members of STEW (Nisi Shawl, Michael Ehart, Mike Canfield, Doreen Mitchum, Robert Kruger, Victoria Garcia, Elizabeth Coleman, Kristen King, and Yang–Yang Wang) suffered through all of these stories and improved them with sage advice and zany ideas. Great thanks are due to editor Deb Taber, proofreader Roger Ivie, and artist Chris Stewart who captured the mood perfectly with his cover design.

The author regretfully assures the reader that actual research occurred in the writing of these stories, and that some of them are based on real events. The reader is invited to guess which ones. (Please keep in mind the US Government was involved most of the time.)

S. Chase

Even though the demands of secrecy have concealed these exploits from the public eye, the Bureau has influenced many historical battles—always defending the home dimension and surface life from dangers that lurk below, or between, or inside the calm veneer of everyday life. Even during WWII…

THE INSPECTION

Lieutenant Commander Gus Morton glared at the radioman hovering in the doorway of his tiny cabin. He waited for him to speak, and then noticed Molumphy's usually expressive face was slack. He had both hands raised in front of him as if he were holding a piece of paper—but Molumphy's hands were empty. Which could only mean one thing.

With an effort, Morton bottled his temper. Snapping at Molumphy would make him lose the vision.

"Message for me?" he said in what he liked to think was a gentle tone.

"Um, yes, Cap'n." The vacant stare continued. God, he hated this. But how many sub captains had radiomen who could receive messages that hadn't been sent yet?

"Why don't you read it to me? My eyes are tired." That worked. Molumphy looked down at the nonexistent typewritten sheet.

"USS *Fintan* report NSB New London for inspection and refit by 05-15-43."

Don't yell at Molumphy. Don't yell at Molumphy. Morton found himself gripping the edge of the tiny Formica-covered desk so tightly the edges cut into his fingers. "Thanks, Molumphy. Carry on." Panic bubbled through him, first immobilizing him and then launching him through the door where Molumphy had stood. He whacked his head painfully on the low lintel. "Dammit!" Morton rubbed his forehead until the stars faded. "Saunders! Where the hell is Saunders? How can that giant hayseed hide in a sub, anyway?"

"XO's up top, Cap'n," a grimy Wogan volunteered. "Cook's girl is payin' us a visit."

Morton swallowed another corrosive burst of profanity, spun on his heel, and darted back into his cabin. The precious, flimsy wooden box in his kit had only one cigar left, and he hesitated before grabbing it. He inhaled the rich, pungent aroma of tobacco wistfully, wishing he had another option. His last Cuban! But a deal was a deal, and she'd earned it. Plus, as the Germans had learned, it was a bad idea to piss her off.

He stuffed the cigar in his front pocket to climb the conning tower ladder. Flinging open the outer hatch, he tripped on the sill and nearly fell flat on the narrow deck. "SAUNDERS!" he screamed, in the general direction of the knot of crew gathered at the bow. "Do I have to fight the entire war by myself? And who authorized a party, you idiots? We've got work to do!"

Saunders slouched over, the sleepy grin on his face undiminished by Morton's accusations. "Just saying hello to Mitzi, Captain. What's the drill? Mitzi's people say the sea is clear for miles."

"Well that's one bit of good news. Which doesn't make up for the fact that we will be ordered back to port in less than a month. *For inspection.*" Morton was gratified to see the grin on Saunders's face vanish. At least *someone* else grasped the danger.

"Molumphy got a future WARNO, sir?"

"Correct." Morton looked about the top surface of *Fintan*, hoping for inspiration. Unfortunately he caught sight of the symmetrical, curved pattern of indentations along the shield piece of the deck gun. It was quite clearly a bite mark from something with a three-foot-wide jaw and teeth that could leave holes in steel. "Gaah! How the hell are we going to explain *that?*"

"Storm damage," Saunders said, making a swinging motion with an invisible hammer. "Just make it a little bit worse; nobody will notice."

"Some storm! And what about the rest of the ship? Those things had claws too. We need to check under the waterline." And if it hadn't been for Mitzi and her people, *Fintan* and crew would have been just another missing sub chalked up to the Nazis. Reminded of his duty, Morton made his way to the bow and the crowd of sailors still gathered there. Cookie was flat on the deck and apparently arm wrestling Mitzi. She was winning.

Mitzi looked up and grinned as Morton approached. Morton tried hard not to shudder, but she *did* have an awful lot of sharp teeth. Whoever had written the legends of mermaids either had left some important details out or hadn't met Mitzi's branch of the tribe. Her scaly section was more like an armored alligator than a fish, too, but from the look in Cookie's eyes, he didn't see anything amiss in his girlfriend. To be fair, Cookie was no movie star himself.

Morton touched the brim of his cap politely. "I am pleased to see you are none the worse from your exertions in the recent fight, ma'am," Morton said, reaching for the cigar in his pocket. "We couldn't ask for better allies. On behalf of myself and the crew of the *Fintan*, please accept—"

Mitzi lunged, snagging the cigar in her mouth and diving over the side, slapping the water with her tail with a resounding splash. Morton checked his fingers for blood. He'd held the cigar by the very end for precisely that reason. Mitzi *loved* cigars, even though she ate them rather than smoked them. Something like catnip for mermaids.

"Got some bad news for you, Cookie. We're heading back soon. I'll need you to break the news to, uh, Miss

Mitzi when she calms down."

"No prollem, Cap'n. Her 'n her people can follow, easy."
At least that's what he thought Cookie said. He had some
ungodly Southern accent combined with a twice-broken
jaw, which made him completely incomprehensible at
times.

Morton's temper started to boil again. "That's what I'm
afraid of, Cookie. What if somebody saw her? The navy is
absolutely certain mermaids don't exist! We don't need
them poking around to see what else they missed!"

He stomped off, yelling for Saunders to follow him. A
sudden strong wind swung the hatch door into his face
when he opened it, and he swore. Back in his cabin, he
scrounged up a tablet of lined paper and a pencil. Saunders
followed shortly afterward, oozing his tall frame through
the narrow door and avoiding the low lintel with an ease
that never failed to irritate Morton. It wasn't fair. The man
was taller, but it was always Morton that was hitting his
head on things.

At his gesture, Saunders shut the door and sat on the
bunk. "We've got plenty of time to hide the damage,
Captain. What are you worried about?"

Morton glared at him. "I'm making a list. Ivek Siggurson,
our shipwrecked Viking, for one. Then Mitzi and her
people. And what if Fluffy follows us home? He's getting
pretty big now and shows up nice and bright even on
normal sonar. Then there's Molumphy and his crystal-ball
brain, the fact that Wogan can now see in the dark, and, oh
yes, we've expended eight torpedoes against a kraken, a
giant sea serpent, a phosphorescent pirate ship, and a horde
of nameless scaly horrors of the deep but *not* German subs.
Plus the crew took part in an actual boarding action, led by
the aforementioned authentic, genuine Viking. I *am* looking
forward to writing up my report. How about you? They'll

set aside a whole wing in the mental hospital just for us!"

Saunders waved his hand. "Siggurson will do whatever you tell him to, Captain. According to Olsen he thinks you are a warrior sent by the gods or something. So we put him on an island and wave good-bye. Not like we can put him back on that sinking longboat, right?"

"I hate to abandon him," Morton grumbled. "He's a good fighter. Berserked that first time he experienced depth charges, but sound man, sound. But he's not on the crew list. What about the rest?"

"Molumphy—we'll give him some morphine and say he's got, oh, I don't know, recurring laryngitis? They won't keep us in port forever; war's still on last time I looked. I'll remind Wogan to keep quiet. As for the rest," he shrugged, "you've been keeping a second log ever since that storm off Bermuda when things started changing. We just need to come up with a better version for the log you hand in. It's not like we didn't sink plenty of Germans."

"Fluffy got most of them, but I take your point. I just hope nobody intercepted that one ship's Mayday call."

Saunders grinned. "You mean the one where he was yelling '*Mein Gott*, the eyes, the eyes!'? Yeah, that might be awkward. We'll just say he was drunk."

Morton grunted. It might work. "We'll have to make sure the crew knows the official story too. It won't do to have another version floating around. And what about Fluffy? Poor little guy. After we killed his mother it just doesn't seem right to put him in danger."

"He thinks *Fintan* is his mother now, but he's getting big enough he'll be heading out on his own soon. He's a *kraken*, for heaven's sake. We're not feeding him enough." Saunders cocked his head. "That's not what has your tail in a knot, Captain. What's the real problem?"

Morton sat silently for a moment, staring at the

bulkhead. He felt cold. "I'm worried about *Fintan*," he said finally. "If they ever find out what she can do, they'll take her apart, down to the last rivet. Just to find out what makes her tick. After all she's done for us, how can I let that happen?"

Saunders looked dubious. "She's a good sub, sir, but what's so special that would get noticed?"

"The Bermuda storm changed *Fintan* too. I think it was the lightning. Never seen it that color before, and it hit smack on the tower. Sure, Molumphy had his little foggy moments before that, but he never got radio messages from the future. I swear the radio changed to pick things up that only he can hear. Same thing with Fluffy. First off, remember how the engines died and wouldn't restart? Just when the mother kraken was nearby and we hadn't figured out the sonar profile? And then when she was dead the hull made the same kind of noises she had, and Fluffy didn't attack, just snuggled up and hung on to the tower. And the time we rocked hard, with the sea smooth as glass, and Cookie fell overboard right near Mitzi's lagoon and she saved him? The sonar alone would be bad enough. It's so accurate you can practically see the serial number on the enemy propellers!"

"Yeah, the sonar. You're right, they'd notice that. And how quiet the engines have gotten. The Germans can't pick us up at all. OK, what's our story?"

For the next two weeks Morton rarely left his cabin except to inspect the "repair" crew's efforts. Between him and Saunders they had cobbled together a sequence of events that covered all the damage they couldn't cover up, the torpedoes expended, known German ships sunk, and the few encounters with other US submarines. Then, fueled by some of Cookie's extra-thick coffee, Morton laboriously copied the details into the official log. He diluted the ink in his pen progressively so the text wouldn't look so uniform and even wrapped his fingers to make his handwriting shakier for a few entries ("depth charge attack sustained, minor injury").

They'd found a nice island off the main trade routes for Siggurson. Olsen, the only one who understood even a little of what the time-traveling castaway said, confided that Siggurson thought he was being left behind because he wasn't good enough to go to Valhalla with them. The Viking had looked quite doleful until Morton, racked with guilt, gave him his own hat. ("Service cover washed overboard in storm.")

By then the real radio message had been received. Cookie made a big pile of rancid Spam, Fluffy's favorite treat, and they fired it out the number two torpedo tube at maximum pressure. A lump in his throat, Morton watched the baby kraken swim happily after it and ordered the ship rigged for silent running, maximum speed. Mitzi had said she'd keep an eye on Fluffy. Morton hoped he'd be OK and wouldn't forget how to distinguish US subs from German ones.

Meanwhile, the officers had been drilling the crew on their stories. Morton kept hearing the conversations, and his nervousness increased.

"No, Gruner, we went over that. You got your injury when the torpedo slipped in the rack. *We never boarded any ships*, got that? And you didn't follow a Viking up a rope to do it either."

"Mewhinney, you did not train Fluffy to attack anyone speaking German. Fluffy doesn't exist. Review your battle cards again, OK? Fluffy NEVER HAPPENED."

When *Fintan* was only half an hour out from the slips, Molumphy reported for his morphine shot. The pages of the real logbook had been carefully hidden in a false bottom of Morton's trunk and the rest of the sub completely sanitized. They'd tried to deliberately detune the sonar, but it kept drifting back to the fine detail setting. Morton shrugged, resigned. He'd just have to hope nobody turned it on while the sub was docked. Then he had to go ashore.

The inspection was thorough, but the crew's countermeasures worked just as they had planned. Aside from mild grumbling at how much damage the hull had taken (some of it carefully applied by the crew) the inspection team showed no sign of suspicion. Shaky with relief, Morton sent the crew off for some well-deserved liberty, with Saunders riding herd on them to make sure alcohol didn't loosen their tongues. He remained behind for the inspection board debriefing.

When he was summoned, Morton was surprised to see a civilian present in the room, a man with thinning grey hair, but the rest of the board ignored him, so Morton did too. The first part of the inspection board was routine, and he started to relax. He'd spent so much time memorizing the fake story it all flowed naturally.

"So, how was it you spent nearly a year without coming back to base?"

Ooops. "We wanted to stay in the fight, sir. Why waste time in transit when we could be supplied at sea?" That had taken some effort to pull off, and a few of Molumphy's future intercepts. Especially getting provisioned only at night. He *really* didn't want to remember loading the torpedoes by hand either, but they had done it.

"You had some unusual requisitions too. A whole *crate* of Spam?"

Beads of sweat formed on his forehead. "My crew enjoyed it, sir. I felt morale was improved." *My crew that had tentacles certainly enjoyed it...*Morton heard mutters along the lines of, "only sub in the fleet that can say that," but no further questions followed on that topic.

"I did not see any notation about training and advancement work. While the war is going well, you really must think about your crew and continuous improvement. The Hun will fight to the end! But I see that you have done fairly well for yourself," the senior officer said, looking sour. "The Germans appear to be avoiding your sector now. In fact, a report has surfaced one U-boat captain was shot by the SS for refusing to patrol there. I don't place too much reliance on that story, since they claim he cited 'monsters' as the reason. Someone in Washington believed you're behind it, though, since you have been put in for some medals. I suppose the paperwork will be along soon."

"Thank you, sir," Morton said, stunned. "I...I must say, none of it would have been possible without the superior abilities and courage of my crew." *And my sub. And Siggurson. And Mitzi. And Fluffy.* He lifted his chin. "It is my honor to serve with them."

Although he had not been officially dismissed, the board was shuffling papers and chatting in a way that clearly indicated the questions were over, and he felt himself relax. Then the civilian spoke up.

"You were assigned the area near the Bahamas, correct?" Morton nodded, feeling his stomach clench. The board was again pretending the civilian wasn't there and hadn't said anything. What was going on? "Did you see anything...odd during your patrols?"

"Could you be more specific, Mr...."

The man ignored the hint. "Oh, say, unusual weather, strange ships...squid of unusual size?"

Panic gripped him, tightening his throat so much he could barely speak. "Saw lots of Germans," he gasped. "That's what I was looking for. Not on a cruise. No time for sightseeing." *Don't think about Fluffy.*

The civilian looked disappointed but didn't say anything more.

It was late when they finally finished with him, and he walked out of the building into the cool night air. Morton found himself walking along the dock where *Fintan* was tied up, looking just like any other *Turbot*-class submarine. He nodded to the sentry, saying "Just want to give her one last check." When out of sight, he laid a hand on the conning tower. "I think we fooled them, old girl. You're safe." The relief he felt was profound. Now he was tired, and all he wanted was a large drink at the O club and a bed that didn't have metal walls on either end.

The sentry saluted as he growled, "Keep a good watch on her; she's been through a lot," and he walked away. He thought he knew the shortcut to the O club, but the warehouses all looked the same in the dark, and he soon realized he was in the wrong area. Then he saw car headlights and quickened his step. He could ask for directions.

But when he got close enough to ask, the shadowy figures weren't wearing uniforms. "This area is closed—" Morton started to say, but two of the men just picked him up by the arms and carried him off.

One of the shadowy men opened a warehouse door. The warehouse was full to the rafters with mysterious wooden crates, all unlabeled. "Dammit, wrong door. Sorry, bud," the man said to a fellow in dungaree coveralls, pushing a crate with scorch marks on the side.

Morton struggled but to no avail. "What the hell do you think you are doing? Who are you people? Saboteurs? You'll never get away with it, and I won't tell you anything!"

The next door they tried showed an empty space, except

for two people—the man with thin grey hair who had been at the review board and the other, strangely, a woman who looked exactly like a middle-aged office secretary, down to the purse and the glasses on a chain about her neck. She was holding a clipboard and looking at him over the glasses with a faintly disapproving expression. The iron grip on Morton's arms released, and he looked back. Two burly men in trench coats and hard expressions were between him and the door.

"What's going on here?" Morton snapped.

The grey-haired man spoke. "Lieutenant Commander Morton. We want to talk to you about your recent activities. The *true* version, if you please. We intercepted a transmission from a German ship that had sighted an Allied submarine."

"Well yes, but—"

"The message included *Fintan*'s hull markings."

"I'm sure there's a perfectly reasonable—"

"And a report of an extremely large dead sea creature that looked like an armored squid in the same area."

Panic spiked. He hadn't fooled them after all. "I already told the board everything. If you don't believe me, check my log. Besides, how do I know *you* aren't Germans?"

The man sighed. "This is a bit irregular, I agree, but we are not German spies. Secrecy, however, required our somewhat forceful invitation. Allow me to show my identification." The papers he presented looked official enough, and they weren't in German.

Morton glared at the man suspiciously. The review board hadn't mentioned that transmission. How had these people known? Why were they here? "I've never heard of this Bureau of Sub-whatchamacallits. Is it connected with submarines? The War Office? What do you want from me?"

"We want to offer you a job."

"I'm not at liberty to accept. As a naval officer, in a time of war—"

"Yes, well, you may have started another one. Not your fault, really, but I suppose you didn't notice the mark on the side of that kraken you took out, did you? Now Atlantis thinks we're attacking them, and we really can't have that spill over into the *other* war. The paperwork alone would be horrendous." The man leaned closer. "We need you, Morton. You, and your crew—*all* of your crew, and your submarine. *Especially* your submarine."

Morton gulped. They knew about *Fintan*. "Who's 'we'?"

The man smiled. "The Bureau of Substandards. And you and your crew will fit in rather well."

The core strength of the Bureau is in its highly capable and supremely talented employees. Finding such unique individuals is always a difficult task, and then there is the training itself...

THE CORRECT WAY TO FILL OUT
FORM PCR-103-U

<u>Section 3.a Describe Precipitating Event</u>

Boris Niels dabbed at an incipient drop of sweat with his handkerchief and looked around, hoping he would see something familiar. The ancient linoleum squares were exactly the same depressing color as they were in the hallway outside his office, and grimy with dust in the same way, but it was not his hallway. He wasn't even sure it was the same building. All of the doors were wood, thickly coated with multiple layers of government-issued paint, and labeled with sequences of numbers and letters that would presumably thwart any spies that penetrated the outer defenses of the Bureau of Substandards in search of a particular location. They had certainly thwarted Niels.

It's only my third day on the job, he though morosely, and wiped his forehead again. Somehow the building air conditioning was able to cool the interior while simultaneously retaining all the humidity, which was a violation of Boyle's law and a few zoning ordinances. *I can't afford to be lost. What will Director Bunsford say?*

Director Bunsford had hired him, even though Niels could see no reason for the Bureau of Substandards having any use for an easily distracted forensic accountant. He'd even worked up the courage to say as much, but Bunsford had dismissed his concerns with a swirling sea of sonorous, half-muffled, and incomplete phrases about potential and resourcefulness. Niels felt like he was being submerged in marshmallow. Director Bunsford gave the impression of marshmallow in his appearance as well, as if it featured in some distant branch of his family tree.

He'd also mumbled something about "seeing where you fit in first" when Niels had asked about his duties. So, Niels had spent his time reading the binder full of department rules and procedures that had been issued to him by the fearsomely efficient Miss Adenaur. He'd even had to sign for it, and he felt a little frisson of excitement when he saw the official government header and warnings against removing it from the building or communicating its contents to any individual not cleared to receive its secrets.

The excitement swiftly waned in the days that followed. Niels sat in his bare, dusty office on a hard wooden chair, in front of a massive metal desk that looked like it had a secondary function as a bomb shelter, and tried to work his way through the binder. At noon he ate his bologna sandwich, still at his desk, and tried to read more. The dust was bothering him, and with a feeling of adventure he decided to look for a vending machine. It was, after all, he reasoned, an office building, even if it was a government office building, and office buildings had vending machines. With cold drinks in them. Maybe even a grape soda. Niels was very fond of grape soda, a fondness not shared by whoever usually stocked vending machines.

He had wandered up stairs and through hallways, now thoroughly lost, but he had decided, with a shrug, if he was lost he might as well stay lost until he found a vending machine. Then he would be lost with a drink. A cold, richly grape-flavored drink. He could almost taste it. And why hadn't he seen anyone else? The doors were closed and he didn't dare knock and disturb anyone, but surely there would be other people working in the department and walking about? Now that he thought about it, in the three days he'd worked here the only people he'd seen were

Director Bunsford, Miss Adenaur, and a janitor mopping the hallway.

A barely audible humming noise alerted him, the distinctive sound of a mechanical apparatus possibly employed in cooling drinks. Niels rounded the corner of yet another identical hallway, and there it was. An ancient vending machine, the kind that dispensed glass bottles from a rack. The bottles were held in place with wire clamps like the business end of a a mousetrap. The glass door was dusty, but Niels could see the bottles and a feebly flickering red light next to the "No Change" sign. Well, he always carried enough coins to make change for any value, so that should be no problem. He drew a breath. One of the bottle caps was purple. Could it be?

He fed in the requested thirty-five cents, marveling that the price was old-fashioned too. They were charging a dollar and a half at the airports, and they didn't have grape soda in glass bottles. The bottle, once he wrestled it free from the wire trap, was icy cold. Niels popped the metal cap off with the opener fastened to the side of the vending machine, and out of habit, checked the coin return slot. There was a coin in it.

Even cheaper than thirty-five cents! rejoiced Niels, and he held up the coin to see how much he had saved. It was hexagonal, a soft, frosted gold color, and he couldn't read the writing or recognize any of the symbols on it. It wasn't American. He wasn't even sure it was human.

Section 3.b List All Incidents Observed and Actions Taken (use additional paper if needed)

By the time Niels found his way back to familiar ground he had drunk all the grape soda and was thirsty again. The janitor was still mopping the hallway, and Niels frowned, looking at his watch. He'd been gone nearly an hour, and the guy was still mopping the same bit of floor? He glanced out of the corner of his eye. The janitor was hunched over, had hairy eyebrows that blended seamlessly with his shaggy hair, and wore a coverall with what looked like oil stains scattered over most of the surface. Niels shrugged. Perhaps it just took him that long to mop.

The strange coin weighed heavily in his pocket. Maybe it was gold. Maybe it was an archaeological artifact, put in by mistake by an absent-minded professor. Who just happened to visit the Bureau of Substandards on his way to report on his findings from an ancient Mayan tomb. Niels sighed and decided to seek help.

Miss Adenaur was typing, on an actual typewriter, a prim and somewhat disapproving expression on her narrow face. Her grey hair was pulled back in a tight bun that was probably bulletproof. The sweater around her shoulders was precisely arranged and fastened by the top button, leaving her arms free, and she had her half glasses perched on her nose, with a chain of faded plastic beads dangling from them and around her neck. Her resemblance to his third-grade teacher was uncanny.

When Niels approached her desk, she looked up and gave him an impatient glance over her glasses. "If you need to see Director Bunsford, he is away at an off-site meeting and won't be back until tomorrow," she said.

"Er, no. That is, I was hoping you could advise me on what I should do with this," he said, and showed her the odd coin. "I found it, and it looks like it might be valuable."

To Niels's great surprise, Miss Adenaur stopped typing and stared at the coin, then at him. She looked shocked. "Where did you find that?" she snapped.

"It was in the coin return of the vending machine

upstairs," Niels said, blinking. That had not been the reaction he was expecting.

"Nonsense. We don't have vending machines in this building."

Niels held up the empty grape soda bottle. Condensation was still visible on the outside of the bottle, and a small dribble of purple liquid was rolling around inside. Miss Adenaur took the bottle gingerly and inspected it through her half glasses. Now she looked worried. "I think you had better show me this vending machine. I wish the director was here," she muttered, removing the paper she had been typing with a zip of the roller and closing it in a safe marked "Classified." She took a crowded ring of keys from her desk drawer and placed them in a large white purse with metal corners. She shooed Niels out of the office and locked it behind her. "All right, where is it?"

Not knowing what else to do, Niels went back down the hallway, attempting to recreate his path. As they walked past the still-mopping janitor, Miss Adenaur said irritably, "I don't know how there could be any unexpected vending machines in this building. We don't get any deliveries for them either. If someone has installed one without the director's permission, we need to find out who did it." The janitor looked up at her through shaggy brows and then returned to his mopping.

Niels went up stairs and down hallways, not seeing the vending machine and painfully aware of the growing expression of skepticism on Miss Adenaur's pinched face. All he had wanted was a grape soda. He could use another one now, with all this stair climbing and walking. Cool, refreshing, rich grape soda....

He turned the corner, and there it was. Still humming away contentedly, with frost on the glass door coyly hiding the bottles inside.

Miss Adenaur gasped and strode indignantly to the machine. "How *dare* they!" she said, her voice quivering. "It's very old. I haven't seen one like that for years. I didn't know they were still in use," she added thoughtfully. She placed her half glasses firmly on her nose and gave the vending machine a close inspection. "The director should know about this," she said slowly, as if she was worried.

"It's just a vending machine," Niels said. "Why is it a problem?" There was still a grape soda inside, and he fed more coins in. "Would you like something, Miss Adenaur?" He pulled out his grape soda and set it on top of the machine.

"Does it have anything diet?" she asked dubiously. "Oh, there. That one, please." The top was a shocking pink. Niels pulled it out and handed it to her, noticing as he did so the "No Change" light had gone out.

Miss Adenaur took a careful sip. "It certainly *tastes* like soda," she conceded.

Niels suddenly had an idea. The strange coin had gone through the machine because it couldn't make change. But now it should work. "I wonder what this will do?" he said, and took out the gold coin.

"NO!" shrieked Miss Adenaur, but it was too late. The mysterious coin made a solid chunking noise as it descended through the vending machine—and then everything stopped being normal. The machine stretched and expanded like taffy, multicolored lightning spreading over it and through the air like very expensive special effects. Niels felt as if he were being turned inside out and then back again. *This is much better than a 3-D movie.*

Suddenly the special effects stopped. The dingy government-issued hallway had vanished, replaced by a rocky cavern lit by giant wrought-iron torches with lots of spikes coming out of them. Niels and Miss Adenaur were standing on a circular stone platform inscribed with strange symbols very similar to the ones he remembered on the gold coin.

Standing around the stone platform were several scaly, monstrous individuals with horned helmets and armor and swords and...Niels blinked. Several scaly, monstrous *horned* individuals. "Ooops," he said.

The creatures moved forward, gripping their weapons and grinning in an unfriendly way. Miss Adenaur screamed and threw her diet soda at them. Immediately the monsters howled in agony, slapping where the soda had splashed them and crashing into each other trying to get away. Niels saw a tunnel off to one side and grabbed Miss Adenaur's arm. "Run!"

They ran until Niels had a stitch in his side and was gasping for air. All he wanted was someplace to hide. Every time they saw one of the creatures he'd dodge down a side tunnel; soon they were hopelessly lost. The tunnels were damp and moisture dripped from above. Niels stepped on something strange and squishy that gleeped and then went silent.

"In there!" whispered Miss Adenaur, pointing to an opening in the tunnel wall. Cobwebs draped the edges of the opening, and when Niels took a cautious look, the small room appeared unoccupied.

"What was...who...where *are* we?" moaned Niels. He sat down on a dusty, iron-bound chest. "Am I really seeing these things? Or was the grape soda past its sell-by date?" He grimaced, recalling his second soda was still on top of the vending machine—assuming the vending machine hadn't eaten it when it morphed. He could use a grape soda now.

Miss Adenaur was gasping for air too, but she did not

seem too distressed. Niels stared at her. A trickle of grey was running down her face, and a splotch of hair now showed a different color. A light gold color.

"You dye your hair?" he said incredulously.

Miss Adenaur glared at him. "What a rude thing to say! I certainly do not *dye* my hair. I merely...color it."

"You color it. Grey. Why?"

She sniffed. "Bureau of Substandards dress code for administrative assistants, Mr. Niels. We strive to keep a certain appearance at all times. I'm not really a full admin; I'm just filling in for Miss Gruntheiss while she's on vacation. She thought I looked too young for such a position of responsibility, so she suggested the hair color. I suppose I should have spent the extra to get the waterproof version." She shivered and put her arms through the dangling sleeves of her sweater. "I don't think we are in the Bureau building anymore, do you?"

"Well, the tunnels are certainly not ADA compliant," Niels said. "And I think the fire marshal would have multiple seizures about the torches everywhere. So, no."

"Is that what you were thinking about while running and dodging those...things?" Miss Adenaur said, admiringly.

"I have a tendency to get distracted under stress," Niels admitted. "That's what lost me my last job." He peered out the doorway. Shadows moved in the distance, and he drew back.

"And what was your previous job, Mr. Niels?" Miss Adenaur dusted a corner of the chest with her handkerchief and sat down.

"Forensic accountant with the DA's office, organized crime division."

"Oooh, how exciting! Gangsters! Did you catch any?"

Niels winced. "Not exactly. Well, it didn't go to trial."

"Why not?"

"He blew up. I *know* I told them about the fireworks; it showed up in the cash flow documentation. He was buying just enough each time to avoid triggering the explosives mandatory reporting—which would have also triggered the storage permit audit—and I pointed this out, but they were looking for tax dodges. So when they went to arrest him, he hid down in the bunker with all the fireworks, and a stray bullet set it all off."

"Well, at least he got what was coming to him," Miss Adenaur said.

"Unfortunately the explosion destroyed most of the evidence, and his family sued for reckless endangerment and felony littering. The DA's office fired me before the investigation found out I was on record as warning about the fireworks." Niels sighed. Somehow, no matter how he tried, it never went right. Just look where a simple grape soda had gotten him. He glanced out the doorway again. This time there was no sign of any activity. "We'd better find a way back to the Bureau."

All the tunnels looked alike, so they wound up following groups of the armed scaly creatures at a careful distance. It took several nerve-racking hours, with the only sustenance some mints Miss Adenaur had in her purse. Unfortunately, when they found the large cavern they had first been transported to, there weren't many places to hide in it. The only place of concealment was a huge, ugly statue behind the stone platform Niels had not noticed earlier, mostly because he was running away screaming in the opposite direction at the time.

"There's too much light," he whispered to Miss Adenaur. "We might be able to sneak by some of the guards if it was just a little darker." She nodded. Niels looked around for inspiration. The clammy tunnel walls had odd, rubbery lichens and other things growing on them, and the floors grew transparent blobs that looked like mushrooms. He stepped on one, and it gleeped with a squish. He tried pulling one of the lichens away but was unable to get any loose until Miss Adenaur took out a metal nail file from her purse. The lichen shrank away from the metal as if it had been burned.

Niels gathered a handful of lichen strands and knotted them together in a loose rope. Then he pulled up a handful of the blobs. He grabbed both ends of the lichen rope, pulled it back with a blob in place, and let fly.

His first attempt missed. The second missed too, but landed much closer to the torch he was aiming for. Luckily, the guard creatures were making so much noise grunting and banging their weapons they did not notice the faint gleeping and squishing.

He hit the first torch. It struggled to stay alight for a moment, then gave up in a puff of green smoke. Another miss, then the second torch went out.

"Oh, good shot!" said Miss Adenaur. A patch of gloom covered their side of the cavern. Niels waited until the guard creatures were involved in some intense discussion before running low for the back of the statue, pulling Miss Adenaur behind him. "Now what do we do?"

Niels placed a handful of blobs on a handy outcrop of the statue, just in case. "There must be a way to use that platform to get back. How else would they be able to get to our world and leave that coin behind?"

"I suppose so," Miss Adenaur said doubtfully. "But when—"

Suddenly the statue they were leaning against started to shake. Glancing out from behind the statue, Niels saw a few puffs of orange smoke and what looked like sparklers. Compared to the amazing lightning of the vending machine, it was hardly impressive. The guard creatures, however, reacted with wails and dropped to their knees, bowing down with scaly arms outstretched. From somewhere inside the statue two beings emerged. They were also scaly, but in a more elegant, snakelike way, and they wore flowing robes.

"It issss time," one said. "The humanssss sssuspect nothing."

"Yesss," said the other. "We ssshall take the key and all dimenssssionss will be oursss!"

The first held up a claw. "Firssst we musst find it. They hide it well. Ssssumon the troopsss!"

As the scaly armored creatures began to fill the cavern, Miss Adenaur tugged on Niels's sleeve. "We have to stop them!" she whispered frantically.

"What were they talking about? Do you know what key they want?"

"Yes! And they can't be allowed to have it!"

Niels carefully looked around the statue. A select group of the guard creatures stood on the stone platform with the two slender snake people. One of the snake people took a staff and whacked the statue on the right knee. The statue's leg kicked out, and as it moved, a rippling disturbance of reality followed with the familiar rainbow-colored lightning threading through it all, engulfing the figures on the platform.

He glanced back at Miss Adenaur. She lifted her large, metal-edged purse with a grim smile. Niels gathered his handful of blobs, readied his slingshot, and jumped up on the now-empty platform. Miss Adenaur followed close behind. From the corner of his eye he saw her swing her purse with a mighty blow as he fired the squishy blobs at the surprised guards, and then the special effects started in. They had done it!

Section 3.c Resolution of Precipitating Event

Back in the real world, Miss Adenaur sped away, Niels desperately trying to keep up. In moments they were back in their familiar hallway, complete with the familiar mopping janitor.

"Joe! Joe!" shrieked Miss Adenaur. "We have a foothold situation. Code nine!"

The shaggy, stooped figure stopped mopping and stood straight. Intelligent grey eyes coolly scanned the corridor, and with a single, fluid motion, Joe flung the yellow plastic "Danger Wet Surface" sign behind them. Niels heard a *whaaauuumm* noise and turned. The yellow plastic sign was creating a shimmering force field, blocking the corridor.

"Orders, ma'am?"

Miss Adenaur rooted in her purse, pulling out the fat ring of keys. "I'm going to use the Form, Joe. Hold them off as long as you can."

"Yes ma'am!" Joe grinned, revealing even white teeth, and rolled up the oil-stained sleeves of his overalls. His forearms were heavily muscled. "I'm on the job."

Miss Adenaur was inserting one of the keys into a door marked "Maintenance." She turned it to the left, waited while counting under her breath, then turned it sharply to the right. "Come on!" she snapped, and jerked her head at the open door. The outside of the door was the usual painted wood, but the inside surface looked like the kind of thing you would see in a bank vault.

"But those creatures—we can't just leave one man to fight them all!" Niels protested.

"Joe is a highly trained Bureau security specialist," Miss Adenaur said. "We don't have much time, and I need you to authorize the Form or it will all be for nothing!"

She grabbed his wrist in an extremely firm grasp and hauled. Niels glanced back, struggling, and saw the janitor's cart had transformed itself into a robot with red glowing eyes and mechanical spider legs, that the brooms and mops had been unscrewed to reveal wicked blades inside, and Joe standing like an Old West gunfighter, a squirt bottle in each hand, guarding the doorway as the door closed slowly behind him.

"What's in those squirt bottles?" he gasped as they ran. This corridor was gleaming and modern, with multiple sensors and devices that scanned them with red laser beams. Miss Adenaur was too busy yelling passwords to reply.

At the end of the corridor was another door, this one with a big steel wheel and heavy metal rods along the surface. There was also a head-shaped depression in the center. Miss Adenaur put her head inside. The door clicked, clanged, and slowly opened. Miss Adenaur shuffled backward, her head still in the depression. "Yu hff tu gu tru fst," she said, her voice muffled. "Gu!"

Niels hesitated. Miss Adenaur kicked him in the shins. Half expecting to be shot with a death ray, he stepped inside the darkness and promptly tripped down a short flight of stairs.

The lights blinked on. "Sorry about that, but the door scanner wouldn't recognize you yet," Miss Adenaur said from the top of the stairs. The door slammed shut behind her, and she ran down the stairs. Niels got painfully to his feet and stared. Inside the room was a building. It looked like several of the small buildings scattered around the grounds of the department, a single-story clapboard structure of WWII vintage. It had a roof and windows. There was even the fifty-five-gallon metal trash can out front.

"Wa...why?"

Miss Adenaur was using another key on her key ring to open the door. "I don't have time to explain. Listen! When you go inside, sit down immediately at the desk. Don't touch anything except the chair, the desk, and the pen. This is important!"

There wasn't much else in the building. There was a door identical to the one they had just entered straight ahead. The desk and chair were on the left side of the room. On the right was a single three-drawer black metal filing cabinet, battered and scratched. On the side were faded yellow stenciled numbers. Miss Adenaur selected another key from the key ring, took a deep breath, and slowly approached the filing cabinet with the key outstretched in front of her as far as she could put it. She unlocked the filing cabinet with great care and opened the middle drawer, taking out a folder that gleamed faintly silver.

Niels sat down at the desk. There was a chipped plastic pen before him, and he picked it up. It warmed briefly and then went cool again.

"I need that," Miss Adenaur said, and took the pen from him. She opened one of the desk drawers and took out an index card box. It was full of the little sticky tape flags that said things like "Please Initial" and "Sign Here." Carefully lifting the form from the folder, she started filling in lines and affixing the "Sign Here" flags.

Niels heard a muffled boom and yelling coming from the corridor. "Um, I don't think we have time for this," he said. "We should go." He looked at the unopened door, estimating the distance. Would there be another exit from the big room, or was it just a closet?

"We have to do this right or it won't work," Miss Adenaur said through clenched teeth. Something slammed into the big steel door, making it bulge. Niels lunged for the door, only to be brought up short by Miss Adenaur's firm grasp of his collar. "Sit and sign!"

Niels sat. "How can I possibly sign for anything? I've only been here three days, and I don't even have an assignment yet!" The form had at least ten pages, and he had to watch carefully to make sure he didn't sign where he was supposed to initial and vice versa. As he turned the pages, the paper began to change, feeling cool and smooth like marble, yet the pen dragged as if it were being pulled in by a magnet. On the last page he had to use both hands, struggling and sweating to make the pen move.

"Hurry! *Hurry!* They've broken through the door!" Miss Adenaur shrieked.

With a supreme effort of will, feet braced against the wall, Niels pushed the pen through the final *s. I am so glad I don't have a name like Hasendorferschein*, he thought, collapsing across the desk.

At first, nothing happened. Then the writing on the page began to glow, then shine, and finally the light was so bright Niels covered his eyes and scrabbled to hide under the desk. Horrible shrieking noises from the scaly other-dimensional creatures outside told him something was finally going right today.

Then the light abated and he crawled out from under the desk. Miss Adenaur was in the corner with her sweater over her head. "I think it's over," Niels said, sounding shaky. He looked outside. The dimensional creatures had melted into a pile of disgusting goo.

"It worked. It really worked," Miss Adenaur said softly, staggering a little. Niels held out his arm. Using each other for balance, they picked their way across the floor and past the crumpled steel door. More piles of goo covered the hallway floor. Niels braced himself for what he might see outside.

Joe the security janitor was sitting against the wall, one eye swollen shut and completely covered in other-dimensional goo. He smiled. "Good job, kid. Lure 'em out and then smack 'em hard. They won't be back for a long time, not this bunch."

"Joe! You're alive!" said Niels, astonished.

Joe sneered. "Take more'n that to do for me, kid. All part of a day's work. And I was almost done mopping that section too. Sneaky bastards. First time they tried a vending machine. Wasn't expecting that."

"What has been happening here?" The rich, sonorous tones of Director Bunsford's voice filled the hall, shortly followed by Director Bunsford filling the hall. If anything, he had gotten more marshmallow-like.

Joe pushed himself up and stood at attention, saluting. "Paranormal Dimensional Incursion thwarted completely, sir!"

Director Bunsford looked about, nodding. "So I see. And the dimensional standard?"

"They never penetrated the final defenses, sir."

"Very good. I shall look forward to your report, but you may take a few hours of rest and get yourself cleaned up. Well, what do you think?" Bunsford gestured at Niels. "Any reservations?"

"Sir, the candidate is a credit to the Bureau of Substandards and exemplifies our finest traditions."

Bunsford blinked, surprised. "I am impressed. Miss Adenaur, do you wish to add anything?"

"He learns and adapts very well, and is extremely quick to pick up on paranormal evidence," Miss Adenaur said primly, refusing to look at Niels.

"Well, then, it would appear the matter is settled."

"*What* is settled?" cried Niels, completely confused.

"Why, my boy, we've found a suitable position for you in the Bureau."

Section 4 Recommendations

"...so I did the best I could to warn Joe without revealing anything to Mr. Niels, and once the dimensional portal was triggered I just followed along," said Miss Adenaur. Director Bunsford nodded.

"Yes, it is a pity we have been so short staffed. Budget cuts, you know," he added to Niels. "We used to be able to train up replacements for upcoming retirements, but these days we recruit only when there is an opening. It can be quite nerve-racking during the changeover. Usually I'm here to pick up the slack, but I had to meet with our alien allies, and it always takes hours. Plus their transporter is optimized for their silicon-based life forms, and it causes terrible water retention in humans. But I'm happy to say you did an excellent job, and the Dimensional Standard was never in danger."

"Sir, what exactly is a Dimensional Standard? And why did I have to fill out a form to defend it?" asked Niels, the new subdirector of Dimensionalities.

"Oh, that's our alien allies again. Terribly concerned with respecting tribal traditions of lower cultures, and so on. They first made contact during the Cold War, and they were *quite* impressed with our paperwork system. Don't have anything like it themselves. So, they triggered the Dimensional Defensive System using a complex bio-sensored artificial intelligence in, er, sheet form. If the correct procedure is followed, the AI activates the system and immediately destroys all entities not in their home dimensions. The Dimensional Standard is a sort of, well, call it a universal remote for dimensions. Very dangerous to let the wrong people get hold of it, I'm sure you will agree."

"But...why do *we* have it? Why don't these superpowerful aliens guard it or something?"

Director Bunsford sighed. "It is more a matter of being *required* to keep it. This is how we earn our allies' protection. There are more threats out there than...but that can wait for later. Suffice it to say, by guarding the Dimensional Standard you are, in effect, protecting the entire planet. Which reminds me, you should sign up for a few of Joe's unarmed combat courses."

Niels digested this in silence for a moment. "You said there were other unusual standards here."

The director nodded. "Yes, and that will be part of your full briefing. You'll be expected to cover sick days and vacations of the other subdirectors, after all. Well, let's see, there's the Fermionic sock—if we lose that, you may as well kiss matched pairs of socks good-bye forever. Then there's the One True Fruitcake, and..."

Social occasions at the Bureau have their own unique challenges that must be met with equal creativity, innovation, and sometimes, alas, alibis....

PLEASE READ THIS MEMO

From: M. Gruntheiss
To: Administrative Staff
Status: Classified/Admins Only
Subject: Upcoming Bureau On-Site Party

1. The task assignments are as follows: U. Labonniere, catering, N. Adenaur, perimeter security, A. Williamsson, decorations and setup, T. Rutherford, cleanup and decontamination.
2. The new subdirector of Dimensionalities, Boris Niels, has not been fully briefed so he has not been made aware of this event. Please do not mention it in his hearing. Off-site training will be arranged for him on the day of the party to prevent any issues. Please remember this is only due to his new hire status and he will be invited to future events, if he survives.
3. Last year we incurred a significant budget loss due to damage of a leased copier that was corroded by salt water. Please do everything possible to keep the frogmen away from expensive equipment, especially when they are drunk. I also hope that Administrative Staff will in future refrain from mentioning traditional party activities such as "photocopying body parts" when frogmen are present.
4. While official style protocol is to refer to frogmen as "historically aquatic humanoid colleagues" no one outside of Upper Management does so or is even

aware of the terminology. To prevent confusion the unofficial term will be used throughout this document. Also remember that the frogmen are valuable assets to the Bureau and consider us "family," having descended from an early Bureau employee and an allied mermaid tribe. Avoid punching them unless you have no other options.

5. VIP guests from Atlantis will be attending this year. This precludes the attendance of all except fully cleared Bureau employees. The Director hopes that there will be sufficient budget surplus for a potluck picnic at a later date where family members will be able to join in.

⊰◔⊱

[Chat Transcript 15:08:32]

UrsulaLa: She gave me catering! What am I going to do??

NanAd: Somebody has to do it

UrsulaLa: Oh no. She thinks I was the one who told the frogmen about the photocopier. I am in such trouble...

NanAd: Don't panic. If she thought that you'd have been sent to the Arctic Circle to do ice weasel population studies for the rest of your life.

UrsulaLa: The last caterer refuses to come back. He screamed and hung up as soon as I said who I was. The others I know of won't even pick up the phone.

NanAd: Mr. Niels might know of some. I'll ask. One of the gangsters he audited liked to give big parties and he saw all the receipts. Experience with gangsters might be very useful if the frogmen get loose again.

UrsulaLa: And they will, you KNOW they will. Thank you SO MUCH. I owe you one.

꙯☉ꙮ

REQUEST FOR BID
Bureau of Substandards
Budget Purchase Authority 294-393-22956
To: DelAmonicotellio Restaurant and Catering

Requirements:
- 300 guests
- hors d'oeuvres, cheese plates, pastries, foie gras, pigs-in-a-blanket, assorted olives, ice cream, pickled herring
- three (3) do-it-yourself sushi stations
- beverage cart, to include several large bottles of colored water labeled "Rum"

Please respond as soon as possible. Also, it is strongly recommended that any employees delivering or setting up the food should be physically fit and not prone to nervous problems or seizures. Please contact Miss Ursula Labonniere with any questions.

p.s. Can you obtain 2-3 cases of Spam that have exceeded their sell-by date? Don't worry, we won't be eating it—it's for something else. U.L.

꙯☉ꙮ

From: A. Lee
To: M. Gruntheiss
CC: Administrative Staff

Is there any way to make sure the frogmen remember to wear their surface clothes for the party? I understand the Atlantis VIPs are very proper and formal, and might take offense if the frogmen run around like they usually do.

From: M. Gruntheiss
To: Administrative Staff

Addition To Earlier Memo:
A. Lee will be in charge of Diplomatic Deportment and frogman wrangling.

🕐

[Chat Transcript 09:32:43]
NanAd: Oh dear. Lee really walked into that one.
UrsulaLa: She's new. She doesn't know how to make suggestions without being volunteered. Or what the frogmen are capable of.
NanAd: I suspect she's going to figure it out pretty soon, poor thing.
UrsulaLa: I've arranged some decoy "booze" for the party. Maybe they won't get so drunk.
NanAd: Good thinking! I don't suppose we know of any sedatives that only work on frogmen, do we?
UrsulaLa: Dynamite ;-)
NanAd: Ha ha. Seriously, we need to help her. You can't expect a one-rhinestone admin to control a whole gang of frogmen. Can we at least hold the party someplace with doors that lock from the outside?

🕐

SCHEDULE OF EVENTS
Location: Bay 1, Subterranean Submarine Tunnel (SST)
Time: 1800
Classification: Full-time Bureau employees and cleared VIP guests ONLY

1800: Introductory remarks and welcome, Director

Bunsford
  1845: Speech by Atlantis representative
  1930: Precision Mop Drill Team Demonstration, Janitorial Security Staff
  2000: Alcohol cabinet unlocked
  2030: Yodeling competition begins
  0200: Triage and cleanup

❧❦☙

[Chat Transcript 11:04:19]
  UrsulaLa: The sub tunnel! That's BRILLIANT! The elevator between that and the rest of the building is secured, even.
  NanAd: It's all concrete and metal down there, too. Hard even for them to damage the furnishings. Plus, we can use the fire hoses to pressure-wash the whole thing for cleanup.
  UrsulaLa: Maybe we'll pull it off this year!
  NanAd: Don't jinx us!!

❧❦☙

Invoice of Services
DelAmonicotellio Restaurant and Catering
  • Food and Beverage, per bid $1,456.32
  • Emergency Alcohol delivery, $879.00 (including tax)
  • Damage to delivery vehicle (repairable) $2,359.00
  • Replacement of custom, hand-carved sushi tables $3,400.00
  • Mental therapy sessions for delivery personnel $1400.00 (ongoing)
NOTE: In the event that the therapy does not successfully treat our employee's Sudden Fish Syndrome, a disability claim will be filed.

❧✦☙

[Chat Transcript 03:41:26]

NanAd: Why didn't we think to disconnect the phone?

UrsulaLa: Because it's supposed to be internal only. Those stupid giant carp hotwired it. *I* want to know how they climbed up the elevator shaft.

NanAd: Well, I guess the bigwigs from Atlantis won't be back this century. That's a plus.

UrsulaLa: Only one I can think of...

❧✦☙

From: M. Gruntheiss
To: Administrative Staff
Re: Bureau Picnic Canceled

(nothing follows)

The position of subdirector of Dimensionalities is unique in many ways, especially in that the dangers inherent to bureaucracy are not purely metaphorical...

WHERE THE MONEY WENT
(AND WHAT IT DID WHEN IT GOT THERE)

Boris Niels took a firm grip on the handle of the top drawer of the filing cabinet, placed one foot on the front of the middle drawer directly below, and heaved. He strained until sweat beaded on his forehead and ran down his face, which was radiating so much heat he was sure he looked like a tomato. The drawer didn't have the common courtesy to even creak—unlike his left shoulder joint, which did. This was shortly followed by a stab of white-hot agony. He stifled a scream and let go.

Niels crashed to the floor and stared at the ceiling, waiting for the pain to ebb to the point where he could take a breath without whimpering. The dull grey filing cabinet with the stenciled letters "AUTH PERS ONLY" on the front sat inert.

"I *am* AUTH PERS," he groaned. "Look! It says so, right on my badge." Wincing, he got up slowly. "Open sesame?" That didn't work, nor did any of the other magic words he could recall—including the ultimate magic word, "Please?" He had a key for the lock, and he could hear it unlatch, but he still couldn't open the cabinet.

He had to get the drawer open. It held the budget folder, and if he didn't find the previous year's budget, he wouldn't be able to write *this* year's budget, and it was due in less than twelve hours. If he had a budget, he would get an administrative assistant who would, he was sure, be able to explain everything else he needed to do.

Miss Adenaur, for example, would have immediately

figured out a solution. Niels brightened at the thought, then frowned. Just his luck she was out for training. Maybe she would be impressed if he figured it out on his own.

He heard a distant, repetitive *sqeeSquk* noise, getting louder and closer. It stopped outside his office, and the door opened to reveal Joe with his janitorial cart behind him. Joe dropped to a crouch and whipped out a squirt bottle, aiming it at Niels—or more accurately, where Niels had been.

"It's just me!" Niels quavered under his massive metal desk. He'd seen Joe in action before.

"Working late tonight, Mr. Niels?" Joe asked. Niels peeked around the corner of the desk. The squirt bottle was gone, and Joe was calmly reaching for the trash can. "Nice reflexes. You missed a really good self-defense class today—you should sign up for the course."

"I can't sign up until my budget gets authorized," Niels said bitterly, reminded of his troubles. He reached for his jacket, hanging on the back of his chair, and pulled out the request with the yellow sticky note of doom on top, waving it. "Miss Gruntheiss denied my request. Apparently my predecessor used up all the money from last year. And now I can't open the filing cabinet, and...hey! Can you open it? Jimmy it or something? It's stuck."

"I'm not authorized to open any classified document containers, sir," Joe said, crushing Niels's burgeoning hopes.

"Is this any way to run a government agency? Nobody is telling me anything. Why can't someone call the previous subdirector? Where is he, anyway?"

Joe turned and looked at Niels, a feather duster in one hand. "They didn't tell you? We don't know where he is." He grimaced, waving the feather duster. "To be accurate, we don't know where *all* of him is. We did find several pieces, though. Enough that we know he's not coming back alive."

Niels dropped into his chair, all joint pain forgotten. "What happened to him?" Joe shrugged. "Where did you find...the bits?" Joe pointed to the floor in front of the filing cabinet. "Something from another dimension got him? I'm not surprised that stupid thing is a portal. Shouldn't we get rid of it?" Niels asked.

Joe kept dusting. "It's not a portal. We have devices that scan for that sort of thing. The way your predecessor described it, things that get exposed to dimensional fields over long periods of time develop an affinity. Sort of like getting magnetized. Never made much sense to me."

"This dimension stuff is dangerous. Why wasn't I warned? Or given any training?"

"It's not the kind of thing you can train for, sir," Joe said, now sweeping the floor with an old-fashioned dust mop. "Dimensions change, move around, try new hairstyles...that's why we have to find the right person. It's a rare ability and can't be taught. You learn as you go, so the subdirector has to have a natural talent for dimensions. And survival. Good luck, sir. You wouldn't have been picked if Director Bunsford didn't think you could do it. Remember, attack into the ambush, and watch the spiders."

Joe gave the doorknob a final polish and left, the *squeeSquk* of his cart fading into the distance.

Shouldn't that be watch OUT for the spiders? Niels wondered, feeling even more depressed. It would be nice if people didn't have quite so much faith in his abilities, at least to the point of giving more hints. Then he brightened. "I have talent! The janitor said so!" He got back to his feet and gave the filing cabinet what he hoped was a steely glare of extreme competence. OK, what did he have to work with?

The filing cabinet was for classified documents, and

further was only to be accessed by the subdirector or his administrative assistant. Regulations for Bureau of Substandards stated all classified folders had to be placed in the appropriate secure container anytime neither of those cleared individuals was in the room. Maybe the filing cabinet didn't realize he was the new subdirector since the previous one (or remains), and his security badge, were still "inside." So, if the classified folder *had* to be in the filing cabinet, and the folder had his authorization in it, then by dimensional logic the permissions would be inside the cabinet, the cabinet would realize its error and it would open.

Before Niels could think the better of it he grabbed an empty folder with the "Classified" hash marks on the edge, labeled it "New Subdirector Authorization," and put his badge in the folder. Laying the closed folder on his desk, he yawned ostentatiously, put on his jacket, and said, "Guess I'd better call it a night, then." He opened the door, turned off the light, closed the door, and locked it.

Everything went black.

Niels flailed for the door. He would just open it and turn on the lights, and then figure out what happened. Maybe the building lights turned off at a preset time?

The door wasn't there. The floor underfoot didn't feel like recently mopped linoleum either, but—he patted it—stone. Cold, grimy stone. Great. He'd managed to get *himself* in a different dimension, not his badge. "Excuse me, but is there a former subdirector of Dimensionalities here?" His voice echoed in the dark, and he wondered how big a space he'd landed in.

No reply came, but he did hear a sound between a thump and a rustle.

"Hello? Anybody there? I'm Boris Niels, and—"

A bright light appeared in the distance, growing larger. It

aimed directly for him, and he put up his hands to defend himself. Something smacked into his hand. It was his badge, now glowing so brightly he could use it as a small lantern. Niels held it up and looked around. He was in a large stone corridor. Flocks of small, yellow fluttery things huddled in corners. Occasionally one would break free of the group and fly off, making sounds that were remarkably similar to "signature required" or "FYI."

Along one wall were big iron doors with signs over the top. "Documentation," "Procedures," "Dimension Notes," "Joint Projects." And "Budgets."

"Aha!" Niels grabbed the handle of the door to Budgets and tugged. The door creaked open, and a gust of stale air, redolent of mold and bad fish, wafted out. Niels held up his badge. A huge, shambling mass of rot wrapped in tatters of waxed paper moaned and shuffled toward him. Niels slammed the door shut and sprinted for the next one down the corridor. Its label read "Misc."

He peered in. No obvious dangers. The monster was hammering blows at the door to Budgets, which was starting to bulge. Niels darted into Misc. and closed the door softly. With luck, the monster wouldn't be able to tell which door he'd gone in.

Misc. was another stone corridor, but with hallways on either side. The hallways had labels too, and strange creatures wandered along them—but never out into the main corridor. Huge, lumbering things like ambulatory sofas with large brown eyes and the word "MEMO" on their foreheads, dense patterns of text dappling their hides, moved slowly. Transparent grey shapes floated in the air, and Niels eventually puzzled out that they were carbon copies. Directives were similar to the memos, but were sleeker and with sharp teeth. They prowled the hallways and watched Niels carefully.

Niels kept walking. So far, all of the hallways had just held creatures, and although he tried talking to them, all they could do was repeat their own content. The carbon copies were especially boring.

Then he found a hallway with what looked like an old man sitting at a desk in it. The hallway label read "JP 3045." The old man looked up from the book he was reading and gestured for Niels to come in.

"Well, it's about time," the old man grumbled. "I've been misfiled for nearly forty years now."

"Sorry?" Niels said. "What—er, who are you?"

"Joint Project 3045," the old man said. "Of course, you probably won't fund me even if I'm in the right section, since nobody noticed I was missing," he added in a irritated tone.

"Heya!" A figure in motley, complete with a belled fool's cap, zipped up. "New audience! Say, did you know a sucking chest wound is Nature's way of telling you to slow down?"

Niels stared, bemused. "What are you?"

JP 3045 scowled. "Joke folder. Go on, push off. We're having a serious conversation here."

The joke folder just grinned. "Never forget, incoming fire has the right-of-way!" It sped out again.

"Sorry about that." JP 3045 sighed and rubbed his head.

"Why do we have a classified joke folder?" Niels asked.

"We don't. Some nameless fool decided to put his collection of jokes in a classified folder so his secretary wouldn't see the naughty ones. Well, once it is classified you have to specifically *de*classify each item, so it was just easier to keep it classified and hope nobody noticed." JP 3045 gave Niels a look. "So, what brings you here?"

Niels did his best to explain about the budget and the unopenable filing cabinet. "I thought I could get inside

Budget and find the file I need, but there's this monster."

"Oh yes. Heard about that. Old tuna sandwich." JP 3045 rolled his eyes at Niels's expression of shock. "Look, we had a rat problem sometime in the 1930s, OK?"

"Why put it in the classified files then?"

"Because the director at the time issued a memo saying you couldn't eat at your desk, per rat problem. Cafeteria only. Guy heard the door open and stuffed his lunch in the closest place that wouldn't get searched. Sandwich slipped to the bottom of the drawer, and it's been there for years."

"I'm beginning to wonder why I want this job so badly," Niels muttered. "Gangsters are more sensible and have a much firmer grasp of reality."

JP 3045 just smiled. "Which is why you are having a conversation with a planning document. Relax, kid. You've hit a rough patch early on, but you are doing quite well."

"How on earth can you know that?" Niels demanded. "I've only been here half an hour."

"You're still alive." JP 3045 shrugged. "Back to your problem. Since I've been stuck here in Misc. I'm a bit out of the loop. I don't know what happened to the last budget. Remember, though, you are the subdirector. You have a lot of power here. Unfortunately, not over old tuna sandwiches. You're going to need to figure out a way to take that thing down before you can proceed."

Niels sat on a corner of the desk and pondered, while JP 3045 folded his hands and waited patiently. Something JP 3045 had said...about a memo. Those lumbering beasts were memos.

"I can refile stuff, right?"

JP 3045 nodded vigorously. "And I sure hope you'll see fit to refile me."

"I will, but right now I need your help. I need to find a specific memo. I sure hope they didn't clean this thing out too much."

JP 3045 looked taken aback. "That's a lot of folders to search. The memos aren't all here in Misc., you know."

Niels got up and headed for the corridor. "Then I'll need a lot of helpers. Come with me. Joke folder!"

The figure in motley zipped up and stopped in front of him. "You *want* me?" it asked incredulously.

"How many jokes do you have?"

It grinned. "Hundreds, boss. Hundreds." The hall suddenly filled with figures in motley. Well, some of the figures were quite voluptuous and not wearing much, but what there was, was motley.

Niels blushed and looked away. "I need you to search for a specific memo. Issued sometime in the 1930s, content forbids eating at your desk, and...do you know the name of the director at the time?" he asked, turning to JP 3045.

"Sorry, I got filed in '46," the old planning document said.

"Never mind, that should give you enough to work with. Go out and bring me that memo!"

The jokes darted away, shouting their fighting cry, "KNOCK, KNOCK!" When they returned they were herding a very large, very confused memo. Niels scanned the text on its sides. There it was...*food is FORBIDDEN in offices of the Bureau.*

When he got out to the main corridor, Niels looked carefully around. The metal door to Budgets was completely off its hinges. Where was the tuna sandwich? The light from his badge only went so far. Then he heard it—the rustle of old, shredded waxed paper. A wave of stench rolled over him, and he whirled and pointed. "FOOD! In the office! Kill!"

The jokes screamed and vanished. The memo went still, then snorted, pawing the ground. The soft brown eyes now showed a disquieting red glint inside. The rotting hulk of the tuna sandwich moaned and flailed, aiming for Niels, but the memo lowered its head and charged, hitting with a resounding smack. The tuna sandwich fought fiercely, but in the end it was no match for an enraged memo.

"Nicely done," said JP 3045, watching the memo placidly chew on a still-wriggling crust. "Now, let's see about this budget problem of yours."

The Budget hallway still smelled like low tide, but no other monsters emerged from the shadows. The side corridors were all labeled by year, and the budgets inside looked like gleaming clockwork robots. Niels reached the end of the hallway, with the last corridor's label showing the previous year. The corridor was completely empty.

"What? But there *was* a budget. How can it be missing?" Niels sagged against the wall. He stared at the year label. It was the right one, no doubt about it. But...

He stared harder. The number was flickering, changing to a different year too quickly for him to read. "Can you make that other year out?" he asked JP 3045.

The old planning document patted at his pockets and produced some reading glasses. "Hmm. Looks like 1952. Why does that year ring a bell? Something about budgets too." He blinked. "Ah, I remember now. It was the one year this department actually ran a surplus. Caused no end of consternation at the time, and I hoped...but I'd been misfiled by then," he added sadly.

Niels went back to the 1952 section. Sure enough, its label was blurring too. The side corridor was filled with darkness, interspersed by flashes of light. When he watched carefully, it was as if the light from his badge only penetrated intermittently. Something was counteracting his authority. He clenched his jaw and walked in.

It looked like a scene from a bad B movie, complete

with the stroboscope effect of a misthreaded projector. A man with long, wild hair wrestled with a clockwork robot that was trying to strangle him, while another clockwork robot stood in a corner, access panel open. The man held a wrench in one hand, and the robot had dangling gears. Whenever the light from Niels's badge faded, a square patch on the man's jacket flared brightly, and the man's body flew into pieces, only to reform at the beginning of the cycle. It was the missing former subdirector!

The man couldn't hear him, no matter how loud Niels yelled, and Niels couldn't touch either of them. His hand hit an invisible resistance when he tried.

"I was afraid of that," said JP 3045. "He tried to go back and take the surplus. He ran out of money for his own budget, didn't he?"

Niels nodded. "So what went wrong?"

"He wasn't subdirector in 1952. No authority then. But he did have authority to access the budget. Problem is, when he tried to remove the surplus he created a time recursion loop."

"And I'm not in that loop because it happened before I was hired, so I can't affect anything inside it with my current authority," Niels said slowly.

"Correct. Only someone with authority over the department could intervene, but they can't get here like you can." JP 3045 spread his hands. "I don't know how you can get out of this one."

Someone in authority. Someone who could deny funds. Someone like Miss Gruntheiss.

Niels reached carefully into his jacket pocket. He wasn't really surprised to feel a soft, feathery body there where the returned letter had been. He pulled it out, and it cheeped, "Denied. Must use current fiscal year funds." He took a deep breath and tossed the little sticky note at the time loop battle.

There was a loud metal crash, a horrible scream he was pretty sure he hadn't made, and sharp, acrid smoke. Niels coughed and waved his hands to dispel the smoke, trying to see what had happened. The former subdirector was gone. The metal budget was twisting and reforming itself, the damage healing while he watched. Soon the budget robot stood whole and still, just like all the others, and the light from Niels's badge was constant. The other budget robot, presumably the previous year's, was no longer there.

"Well, that should take care of the problem," JP 3045 said with an air of satisfaction. "I'll bet that time loop was what was keeping you out of the filing cabinet in the home dimension. What you didn't know was you could have opened it in the few seconds when your authority was valid during the cycle, but it still would have caused problems. I doubt you would have been able to get to that budget to check it."

"So everything will work now? How do I get back?"

JP 3045 raised a bushy eyebrow at him. "I'm just a planning document, son. What on earth would I know about dimensional travel?"

"You know about a lot of other stuff."

He shook his head. "That's from experience. Never been out of this dimension. How did you get in?"

By accident, Niels thought morosely. Maybe if he went back to where he'd started, he'd get an idea.

On the way, he returned JP 3045 to his proper section in Joint Projects, and he thought the old planning document had a tear in his eye at the thought of returning home.

There. End of the main corridor. All normal. Nothing remarkable, no "Exit Dimension Here" signs. Only a black spider with glowing red eyes clicking along the stone floor...

Watch the spiders.

Niels followed the spider to a decorative stone column. It looked solid, as did the wall it was attached to, but when the little spider tapped on the base of the column a section shimmered and vanished. A section about three feet wide and a foot and a half high. Niels lunged for the opening.

He came out in a room full of high-tech monitors and gleaming control panels, staffed by a number of hard-eyed, strong-jawed men in janitorial uniforms. Niels unfolded himself and stood up, brushing several mechanical spiders from his jacket.

"I'm guessing this is the dimensional portal scanning room, yes? I'd love to take a tour, but I have an urgent budget to write. Oh, and could you send Joe to my office with a mop and a body bag? Don't worry, he knows all about it."

Working well with other Bureau employees is crucial to a successful career. Attention to interpersonal relations is strongly encouraged at all levels, regardless of job description. Properly done, the effects can last a lifetime...

ALL ACCORDING TO REGULATIONS

Niels heaved the briefcase up just in time to block the blow, sweat dripping down to sting his eyes. His arms felt like rubber. *Tired* rubber. "Why do I have to do this wearing a suit?" he gasped.

"Gotta train like you fight, sir," Joe said, lifting his combat mop for another try. "Statistically, you are more likely to be attacked while wearing a suit than in exercise gear. Try the swing again. Move with the spin, and the weight will lift your arm on its own."

"So if we train like we fight, why is the briefcase loaded with bricks?"

"Using weighted training tools makes the everyday carry seem light. Plus the additional cardio benefits," Joe added.

Niels dutifully swung the briefcase around, but just as he built up speed, the handle slipped from his sweaty hands and the briefcase went flying across the gym. With a sigh he trudged off to retrieve it.

The Bureau of Substandards gym was quite large and had sections for regular gym-type weights as well as Bureau specialties such as the briefcase training area and the weapons range for the janitorial staff. Located in one of many basements, it was all cinder block painted a pale bile yellow and smelled strongly of old socks and pine floor cleaner.

Niels bent, wincing, to pick up the briefcase. A repeated, regular thwacking sound made him look up. Across the gym in the sparring section, Miss Adenaur was beating the living daylights out of a punching bag with her purse. She was wearing a soft pink sweater set and a tweed skirt, and she looked as gorgeous as she had the last time he'd seen her on the attack.

The briefcase slipped out of his nerveless hand, landing painfully on his toes. Niels yelped. Miss Adenaur glanced over at him and he waved, his injuries and fatigue forgotten. *Wow, she's really good at that!*

"We're not finished yet, sir," Joe yelled from across the room.

For the remainder of the session Niels struggled to keep up with Joe's instructions, very aware that Miss Adenaur might be watching him. He *was* getting better, even if he still was gasping for air at the end, but he lacked her skill.

"Nice job, Mr. Niels. I'll see you next Tuesday, and we can start on umbrella-kata," Joe said. Niels waved one hand weakly, still wheezing, and looked around the gym for Miss Adenaur. She wasn't there. He hobbled out the door and saw her heading down the hallway.

"Miss Adenaur! Wait!"

She turned and folded her hands primly. "Yes, Mr. Niels?"

"You're back! I was looking all over for you when I couldn't find the budget and I *really* needed your advice."

She allowed herself a small smile. "I understand you took care of the matter quite well all by yourself. Joe was certainly impressed. He's always telling me, 'Don't get attached!' but if he's training you himself he must think you have *some* chance."

"Yes, well, I wish someone had told me about the average life expectancy of subdirectors before I signed up—not to mention rogue tuna sandwiches—especially since getting out of one jam just gets me in another. Sure, I got the budget together on time, but now they are saying I didn't follow the correct protocols for declassification—I mean, how do you declassify a *corpse*, for heaven's sake? So now the classified file cabinet has these big medieval chains all over it, and I can't open it without supervision until I've been properly briefed, and if I screw up something classified again I might get arrested." Niels waved his hands in agitation, wincing as his tortured muscles promptly cramped up.

He winced again at the thought that even if he was merely fired rather than arrested, he would not be working in the same building as Miss Adenaur—a perk, he suddenly realized, that counted for a significant percentage of his job satisfaction.

Miss Adenaur looked concerned. "But you have your budget now, right? You can get an admin assigned to you now. We admins are fully trained in all the procedures and protocols."

Niels sagged in relief. "Of course, I remember now. I suppose there is a requisition form? I'll go right up and find it." He sighed. "Right after I get some aspirin. I don't suppose you have any recommendations for admins?"

The little smile on Miss Adenaur's face vanished. "I'm sorry, Mr. Niels. Now if you will excuse me, I must get back to work."

"Oh, right." Niels watched her go, puzzled. She'd seemed so friendly, until...well, he had asked a lot of questions. And she was undoubtedly very busy with other problems than his. He brightened. Maybe he should ask her out for...coffee. Or ice cream. To show his appreciation for her help. Yes, that was what he should do.

He made sure to be in the building foyer at the end of the workday. While he waited, he counted up the number of plaques on the In Memoriam wall that belonged to subdirectors of Dimensionalities. With morbid satisfaction, he calculated his job position accounted for at least 60 percent of the fatalities in the Bureau upper management. The janitors, of course, had the highest overall body count.

Finally he saw Miss Adenaur walking quickly toward the door. She was carrying her large white assault purse, and he made sure to stay out of range as he caught up to her. She might still be displeased with him.

"I was wondering if you might like some refreshment after your exertions in the gym? There's an ice cream place nearby that is highly recommended," he stammered.

Miss Adenaur gave him an uncertain look. "In this dimension?"

"Absolutely. I've been there several times before I even heard of the Bureau."

Her expression cleared. "Oh, good. Yes, that sounds very nice. It's been a long day."

To avoid any further irritation, Niels was very careful to not ask any work-related questions. To his great relief Miss Adenaur became quite genial under the influence of chocolate ice cream with hot fudge sauce and chocolate sprinkles.

"This is *amazing* ice cream," she said, licking her spoon. "How did you hear about this place?"

"Ever hear of 'Fat Tony' Morelli?"

"The gangster?" Miss Adenaur said, giving him her full attention. "Of course!"

"He's a devoted fan. We got him to turn state's witness just by bringing him a quart from this place every week he was in prison. His favorite is the pimento with salted caramel."

"Ohhh..." Miss Adenaur looked wistfully back at the counter. "That does sound good. But I'm stuffed!"

Niels smiled. "We'll just have to come back, then. Perhaps several times, to see if Fat Tony's opinion is supported by the evidence. The blackberry-port ice cream is also quite good."

"And to check for consistency," Miss Adenaur agreed. "I

can see a great deal of research is needed."

Niels was quite happy with the results of the ice cream experiment. The next day he was busy reading in his office when Miss Adenaur stopped by. "The lunch deli had grape soda today, so I got you one," she said with a smile. "And I picked up your mail since I was coming here anyway."

Niels gazed at her with admiration. "Your instincts are impeccable, Miss Adenaur. I was getting very thirsty." He waved at the open folder. "This planning document is a hard slog—but I owe it a favor since it helped me with the budget problem. I figured the least I could do was some preliminary investigation funding, but now I need to know what it is *about*. Somehow that never came up when we were chatting...."

His eye snagged on the large manila interoffice mail envelope. "Oh, maybe that's the request I sent in." Niels opened it and puzzled over Miss Gruntheiss's scrawled note. "Wait, I have to *specify* an admin? I don't know any!"

Miss Adenaur congealed into an icy statue. "You know *me*," she said, her arms folded across her chest.

"But you're too important!" Niels blurted, sheer panic overwhelming him. "I just need someone to keep me out of trouble!" *And I want to take you out for ice cream again. Maybe even a movie.* The last thing he needed now was an HR violation on top of his goof with a classified cadaver.

"You are a full subdirector, Mr. Niels," she said firmly, "and subdirector of Dimensionalities, which is a very difficult post. It's crucial for you to have a good working relationship with your administrative assistant, given the dangers. Other subdirectors might rate a general assignment, but not you. Don't you think we worked well together dealing with those nasty snake creatures?" she asked, looking hurt.

"You were the only reason we survived!" Niels said

fervently. "I just tried to stay out of your way. I didn't do anything useful."

"Oh, don't be silly. You got us out of the snake people dimension, and with plenty of time to stop the invasion." Miss Adenaur looked happy again, so Niels didn't contradict her. She put on her reading glasses and picked up the form.

He peered at her. "Are those new glasses, Miss Adenaur?" They were the same kind of pearlized plastic with the cat-eye shape but had more rhinestones at their corners than her previous pair.

"I was promoted after we stopped the invasion," she said proudly. "All thanks to you. Here, I'll help you with the form. You really shouldn't put this off a moment longer. Who knows what will show up next?"

Niels gave up. He needed an admin, and Miss Adenaur clearly wanted the job...and he'd just have to behave himself. At least he'd get to see her all day.... He sighed. "What do I need to do?"

"Just put my name here on this line. That's Nannette, two Ns, two Ts..."

"Oh." Niels stared at her. "It—it suits you." This was going to be harder than he thought. A pretty face and a pretty name? He felt his face heat up, and he quickly wrote her name on the form without looking at her again. One faint hope remained. "What if Miss Gruntheiss doesn't approve?"

"There shouldn't be any problem; with my promotion my rank is high enough, and with your personal request it should go through immediately. I'll take this in right away." Miss Adenaur swiped the form before Niels could grab it.

Still not looking up, Niels heard the quick step of her high-heeled shoes leave the office. The door closed behind her, and he sagged in his chair. It was all going wrong. He suddenly had an urge to go to the refuge of the classified filing cabinet and ask the wise old JP 3045 for advice, but the massive metal chains were still wrapped firmly around it. No, the only question was if he would get fired before he got his name on a plaque.

He drank his grape soda despondently and flicked through the remainder of his mail. At the bottom was a message from Security and Cleaning Services, notifying him that his issued protective gear was now ready.

Niels trudged over, was scanned and verified and searched at the entrance, and was finally allowed to proceed. Joe was waiting with an assortment of devices intended to protect Niels from all manner of multidimensional threats while appearing to be ordinary, innocent objects. A sad-looking cactus in a pot with "Souvenir of Xopthiloc" on the side was actually a scanning and monitoring device for his apartment. A key fob turned into a giant remote-controlled balloon.

"You need to be alert and on the defensive twenty-four/seven," Joe told him, pointing a finger for emphasis. "A cross-dimensional incursion could happen at any time. And they'll be looking for you in particular, especially since you've been doing dimensional traveling."

"Great. Another job benefit they neglected to mention." Niels picked up some of the other devices. A cell phone that was really a laser weapon, and a music player that was really a targeting computer, electronic shield, fire starter—and could also be used as a phone. He signed for it all listlessly, including a pair of glasses with an X-ray mode, wondering at his lack of enthusiasm. He'd always wanted X-ray glasses. Why did they feel like a disappointment?

"Everything all right, sir?" Joe gave him a concerned look. "They may not look like much, but they are top-of-the-line components. I tested them personally. You have an admin now, right? She can help you practice with them."

Panic surged. "No. Bad idea." He wasn't going to even *touch* the X-ray glasses when Miss Adenaur was in the room.

Joe frowned. "They are all professionally trained. And Miss Adenaur especially—you did get Miss Adenaur, right?" Niels nodded. "She's one of the best."

"She *is* the best!" Niels said, hotly. "That's the *problem*. She's wonderful. I worked at one company where my boss complimented a lady on her hat. By the time HR got through with him he'd sworn off women and joined a monastery in Uzbekistan."

Joe blinked. "Maybe he's happy there."

"His wife wasn't. She sued the company for alienation of affection and won. The judge fined them the minimum amount only because he was fascinated to see a legal fiction named as a co-respondent in a divorce case and wanted to write a paper for a law journal about it. But if I try and get a different admin, Miss Adenaur will be mad at me. I don't know what to do!"

Joe looked thoughtful, rubbing a meaty hand over his jaw. "I see. I think you should talk to Director Bunsford about it. She can't get mad at you if the director rearranges the staff, can she?"

Niels gave him a suspicious glance, but Joe met his eyes with an expression of complete innocence. Well, what did he have to lose?

Niels wasted no time in requesting an appointment. The fearsome Miss Gruntheiss looked at him over her reading glasses, which Niels noticed were covered with rhinestones at the edges, and informed him the director could see him now for five minutes. "Don't keep him any longer," she said, sniffing and returning to her typing. With some trepidation, Niels went into the director's office.

Director Bunsford had apparently been able to avoid using the alien transporter for a while, because he was looking only slightly puffy at present.

"So, Boris, settling in all right? We are thinking of using your budget as an example for the other departments. Would you believe people have to be told to check that their total request actually matches the sum of the individual line items?" Director Bunsford sighed.

"Er, yes sir. Settling in. About that...um, Miss Adenaur...." Somehow Niels stumbled through what he desperately hoped was a diplomatic explanation of his difficulty, all the time keeping a weather eye on the countenance of Director Bunsford. The director remained calm and attentive, and Niels began to hope.

"You never finished reading the manual of procedures, did you? Oh, I suppose the relevant section is in the classified folder, at that. No, I am afraid I see no reason to reassign Miss Adenaur."

Niels felt his stomach drop to his feet.

"You see, Boris, we have a slightly unusual corporate structure here at the Bureau. We've found it suits our needs better. I suppose you think Miss Gruntheiss is my subordinate, yes?" The director gave him an indulgent smile.

"She isn't, sir?" Niels was now completely puzzled. "She's...your superior?"

"In many ways, but not in the manner under discussion. The executive and administrative branches are on completely separate tracks. So, while Miss Adenaur is under the supervision of Miss Gruntheiss, she is *not* under yours. The rules against fraternization don't apply."

Understanding shot through Niels, and he sat up, gloom dispelled. "Really?" he asked eagerly. "I can ask her out and not get fired?"

Director Bunsford beamed. "Precisely. I do recommend you study the relevant section of the manual when you have a moment. Not only do we have separate branches, we, er, promote the development of close departmental teams. Very close. Miss Gruntheiss and I, for example, recently celebrated our twelfth anniversary. It doesn't always work out, of course, but we like to encourage it when we can. And in pursuit of that goal," he said, opening a drawer and pulling out an envelope labeled "Lunch," "we have an informal Interpersonal Development Fund, a.k.a. Date Money. Miss Gruntheiss informs me there is a new gangster movie out, and Miss Adenaur hasn't seen it yet." The director handed over a generous wad of cash. "Don't keep her out too late, now. You both have a lot of work to do still."

"Yes, sir!" Niels said.

He wandered out of the office in a daze. It was just starting to register that he really did have an admin, the *perfect* admin, who not only would steer him through the shoals of Bureau procedure but also miraculously seemed to prefer his company. Now all he had to do was stay alive to enjoy it.

As he walked down the hallway thinking of schemes to entertain Miss Adenaur, something odd caught his eye. One of the large potted plants seemed a bit thicker than it should be.

"Joe?"

The leaves parted. "Damn, sir, you *are* getting good at this! So, how'd it go?"

Niels glared at him. "Very well, as you already knew, and why the hell didn't you tell me yourself? You people take compartmentalization much too seriously."

Joe shrugged. "Interdepartmental operations aren't my responsibility. Your personal safety is. Which reminds me, I need to know what movie theater you are taking Miss Adenaur to."

"I do *not* need a chaperone, and neither does she. You've seen her wield that purse, haven't you?" Niels leaned closer to the plant and whispered, "Don't cramp my style, Joe."

"She'll be distracted by the movie, and your self-defense still needs work," Joe grumbled. "Fine, take this then." He pulled out one of the portal-scanning mechanical spiders. It stood on his palm and saluted Niels with one black, hairy leg.

Niels gingerly picked it up. The spider compacted itself into something that might have been a coin purse, if a coin purse were made out of high-tech carbon composite and had red glowing eyes.

"So if I take this, you won't need to keep me under personal surveillance? I don't want to find out you guys replay our conversations for entertainment during your coffee breaks."

Joe grinned. "I'll do my best not to disappoint you, sir."

"I was afraid of that," Niels sighed. Maybe Joe wouldn't offer suggestions on technique.

Maybe.

ABOUT THE AUTHOR

Sabrina Chase was originally trained as a Mad Scientist, but due to a tragic lack of available lairs at the time of graduation fell into low company and started working in the software industry. She lives in the Pacific Northwest and is owned by two cats.

Further sordid details may or may not be available at her website, chaseadventures.com

www.ingramcontent.com/pod-product-compliance
Lightning Source LLC
Chambersburg PA
CBHW071202130626
46555CB00004B/1552